The Not-So-Pretty Pixies

To Bina,
the best sisterrrr!
—G. S.

DaiSY DREAMER

#4

The Not-So-Pretty Pixies

By Holly Anna • Illustrated by Genevieve Santos

LITTLE SIMON
New York London Toronto Sydney New Delhi

LITTLE SIMON

An imprint of Simon & Schuster Children's Publishing Division
1230 Avenue of the Americas, New York, New York 10020
First Little Simon hardcover edition October 2017
Copyright © 2017 by Simon & Schuster, Inc.
Also available in a Little Simon paperback edition.
All rights reserved, including the right of reproduction in whole or in part in any form.
LITTLE SIMON is a registered trademark of Simon & Schuster, Inc., and associated colophon is a trademark of Simon & Schuster, Inc. For information about special discounts for bulk purchases, please contact Simon & Schuster Special Sales at 1-866-506-1949 or business@simonandschuster.com. The Simon & Schuster Speakers Bureau can bring authors to your live event. For more information or to book an event contact the Simon & Schuster Speakers Bureau at 1-866-248-3049 or visit our website at www.simonspeakers.com.
Designed by Laura Roode
Manufactured in the United States of America 0917 FFG
2 4 6 8 10 9 7 5 3 1
Library of Congress Cataloging-in-Publication Data
Names: Anna, Holly, author. | Santos, Genevieve, illustrator.
Title: The not-so-pretty pixies / by Holly Anna ; illustrated by Genevieve Santos.
Description: First Little Simon edition. | New York : Little Simon, 2017. | Series: Daisy Dreamer ; 4 |
Summary: "In this fourth adventure, Daisy and Posey help a pretty pixie named Twee get to the bottom of a not-so-pretty problem"— Provided by publisher.
Identifiers: LCCN 2017017068 | ISBN 9781481498876 (pbk) | ISBN 9781481498883 (hc) |
ISBN 9781481498890 (eBook)
Subjects: | CYAC: Imagination—Fiction. | Imaginary playmates—Fiction. | Pixies—Fiction. |
Conflict management—Fiction. | BISAC: JUVENILE FICTION / Imagination & Play. |
JUVENILE FICTION / Humorous Stories. | JUVENILE FICTION / Readers / Chapter Books.
Classification: LCC PZ7.1.A568 Not 2017 | DDC [Fic]—dc23
LC record available at https://lccn.loc.gov/2017017068

CONTENTS

☆ CHAPTER ONE ☆

Wipeout!

Clickety-clackety-clickety-clack!

I zoom down the sidewalk on my skateboard. The wind makes my hair fly out of my pigtails, and I have to spit it out of my mouth. *Pfffffftttt!*

"Hurry up, Mom!"

Mom and I are going to school *like always*, and I tease her *like always* because she is a slowpoke. Mom is walking and I'm on my skateboard, so I am wayyyyy in front of her. *Obviously!*

Suddenly a blast of light flashes in my eyes and blinds me! I can't see anything!

"*Aaaaaaaaaaaaaah!*"

Then—*ka-bonkity ka-bonk!*—I fall feet-over-helmet onto the sidewalk. WIPEOUT!!!

I hear footsteps rush to my side.

"Wow!" says a girl from behind me. "Are you okay?"

"Here, let us help you!" another girl says.

I look up and can't believe it! It's that awful Gabby Gaburp and her meanie sidekick, Carol Rattinger. What are *they* doing here? And why are they being so *nice*?

They pull me up and help me dust off. I have dirt all over my knees and elbows, but I don't hurt anywhere. Phew! While I am dusting, I check to make sure they haven't put a PRANK ME sign on my backpack.

Nope—all clear!

I double-check my skateboard in case they did something bad to it. But nothing seems different—the wheels still spin and make an awesome swirly spiral when they turn. There's not a meanie trick in sight.

I'm all, *Huh? These two girls are never nice to me. It's just plain weird.*

"Thanks for your help, I guess?" I say to them. It *was* really nice of them to check on me.

"Oh, Daisy, thank goodness you're okay!" Mom says, finally catching

up to us. I guess I was way wayyy waaaaayyy ahead of her. "You've got to be more careful when you're going that fast, Miss Daisy Dreamer!" she scolds me.

Then she turns to Carol and Gabby.

"Thank you, girls, for helping Daisy! I'm so glad she's all right!"

The girls smile sweetly. I didn't even know their faces could do that!

"No problem, Mrs. D.!" they say, and we all grin at one another.

It feels really weird and strange, but it's nice for a change. And to make things even stranger, Gabby, Carol, and I walk the rest of the way to school together, like we're friends. Did my world just turn upside down?

I mean, I have a big imagination, but I would never ever have imagined *this*.

TNF: Totally. Not. Fair.

Gabby and I always sit at the same table at school. Usually she never looks at me. But today she looks at me a lot. Like, *a lot* a lot. It makes me think maybe I have something on my face. So I rub my face all over, but nothing comes off.

What is going on with her today? I wonder. Something *has* to be wrong. *Obviously.*

So I ask, "What are you staring at, Gabby?"

And she twists her face all funny and looks kind of embarrassed. "I . . . I think you have someone on your head," she says.

I sit right up in my chair. "WHAT?!"
I say, a little bit too loud. I pat my
hair all over, but I can't feel anything.

*What is she talking about? I wonder.
I would know if there was a person on
my head. Obviously!*

I expect her to laugh at me, but she doesn't, which is also weird. All I can think is that it must have been her imagination.

And speaking of imagining . . . I haven't seen my friend Posey in days! I've tried to go to the World of Make-Believe all week but couldn't get in. I miss my very real imaginary friend!

While I am thinking about Posey, a bright light flashes in my eyes *again*, and I am blinded, just like on my skateboard. I rub my eyes and look around to see who did it.

I spy Carol over in the corner. She's tilting her watch to reflect a beam of sunlight right into my eyes!

"Hey!" I shout. "Stop that!"

Everyone turns around and stares at me. Carol, of course, pretends like nothing happened. But I know better, so I point my finger at her.

"So *you're* the reason I fell off my skateboard this morning!" I yell at her. "You did that on purpose, and you were just *pretending* to be nice!"

Carol leans over her table. "DID NOT!" she shouts.

"DID TOO!" I shout back.

Then I whip around and glare at Gabby. "And I bet you didn't see any-thing on my head, either!" I yell at her. "You were just trying to make me look silly!"

Gabby lets out a huff. "You're wrong!" she complains. "And you're not being fair!"

Our teacher, Mr. Roberts, makes a time-out sign with his hands and whistles loudly. We stop yelling. Then

he walks over to my table and asks
what's wrong. I try to explain that
Gabby and Carol are making fun of
me.

"Well, it's not true!" Gabby says
firmly. But I don't believe her for a

second. Then Gabby makes a sad, pouty face, and Mr. Roberts actually believes her!

And what's worse? He says I have to stay after class for yelling, which is TNF: Totally. Not. Fair.

Obviously.

Did You Knock?

The bell rang and everyone got to go except me because I am in trouble. Mr. Roberts is going to get my mom right now, and here I am, stuck in this dumb classroom all by myself. To make matters worse, I can hear kids laughing and having all kinds of fun outside. TNF!

Bonk! Bonk! Bonk!

That's my head bonking the table because I am *B-O-R-E-D*.

"*PSSSSSSST!*"

Wait, what's that noise? I look all around, but nobody's there.

"*PSSSSSSST!*"

Hey, there it goes again! It comes from the window. I squint hard and see nothing but dust particles floating in the light. But then the dust particles start coming together—like magic—and I see a Pretty Pixie!

It's *Twee!*

I run to the window and say hi. It's been a long time since I've seen

anyone from the WOM, and I'm so happy she's here! I hold out my finger like a little perch, and Twee lands on it. She looks at me and frowns.

"What's wrong?" I ask.

And Twee's tiny eyes grow wide. "There's trouble in the Land of the Pretty Pixies!" she says. "I need your help!"

I walk back to my table, balancing Twee on my finger.

"I wish I could!" I say. "But I haven't been able to get into the WOM all week! I draw doors, but none of them open!"

Twee shifts her tiny feet, and it
tickles my finger.

"I can help with
that," Twee says,
like it's no big
deal. Then she flies
across the room,
grabs a sheet of
paper, and slides
it in front of me.
"Just try again,"

she tells me. And now I feel a little
bad for giving up so easily.

I rummage through my pencil case
and pull out a purple marker. I'm just

about to draw a door when I hear a knock from underneath the table.

Rap! Rap! Rap!

I lean over and peer underneath. My pigtails go upside down. I check everywhere, but there's nobody there.

I pop back up, and then a doorbell rings. And rings. And rings.

Ding-dong! Ding-dong! Ding-dong!

The chimes seem to come from under the table too. I look at Twee, and she points to the paper.

"Just draw a door," she urges. "Then maybe you can answer it."

So I quickly draw a door. No sooner

do I add a doorknob than it instantly opens up. And guess who's standing there with his arms crossed? Posey! *Obviously.*

"It's about time!" he says a little grumpily. "I was beginning to think you'd forgotten about me!"

"I would *never* forget about you!" I say. And then I explain how I've been drawing doors all week and how none of them opened.

Posey and Twee shake their heads like they don't believe a word I'm saying.

"Well, did you *knock* on the doors after you made them?" Posey asks.

I scratch my head. "Nope," I say. "I just tried the knobs."

Posey clunks his forehead with one of his hands. "You have to *knock*, silly!" he says. Then he holds one hand to his ear.

So right on cue, I rap on my desk three times. "You mean like that?"

"Perfect!" Posey says. "Knock and the door shall open!" Then he winks at me. "Now let's go play!"

"Sounds good!" I say as I hop up from my table. Then I put my hands over my head, lean over, and dive right through the door I drew on my paper.

Chapter Four

What Now?

Whoa! Everything's upside down! I mean really, actually, truly upside down. I'm dangling from a tree!

"HELP!" I shout, but Posey and Twee are too busy laughing at me. Posey snorts through his nose so he sounds like a rhinoceros, and Twee actually tweets!

TWEET! SNORT! TWEET! SNORT!

I don't think it's funny until *after* they get me down.

"We forgot to warn you—you have to enter the WOM feetfirst. Otherwise you arrive upside down!" Posey points out.

I roll my eyes. "Well, thanks for the heads up!" I say.

Then Twee elbows Posey. "More like a heads down!" she says, and they both start giggling again.

I pull a leaf from my hair. "Don't we have work to do?" I remind them.

Twee claps her teeny-tiny hands. "Oh yes, we do!" she says, beckoning us to follow her. "Now, be careful where you step. Pretty Pixie villages are *tiny*!"

I take all of two steps, and

something goes *squish*! Right. Under.
My. Foot.

"Oh no!" I cry. "I
accidentally stepped on
a mushroom house!"
The Pretty Pixie owner
is shaking her fist and
shouting in a pipsqueak

voice at me. I am just glad she wasn't
inside.

Posey plucks a new mushroom from
the forest floor and sprinkles some
imaginary friend dust on top of it.

"Fixer-upper!" he shouts. And just
like that, the mushroom magically
turns into a brand-new house—only

bigger and better than the one I had stepped on. Posey hands it to me, and I carefully place it on the ground next to the squashed house. The pixie claps her hands in delight.

Reminder to self: Sneak some of Posey's imaginary friend dust. That stuff is *amazing!*

After that, I am much more care-ful about where I step. But now I am watching my feet so hard that—*blammo!* I walk straight into a swarm of angry pixies.

"OWEE!" I cry.

Little leaves flicker against my face.
Tiny fists and feet strike my eyes,
nose, and ears. I even have little pixies
tangled in my hair! And all of them
are shouting at one another.

"WHAT IS GOING ON HERE?"
I yell over the noise.

But nobody pays
any attention to me.

Finally, Twee lets out
an earsplitting whistle.

"SCREEEEEEEE!"

The pixies all stop
talking at once and look
at us. Some mutter an apology. Some
stick out their tongues. Others hiss.
All of them separate into two groups
on either side of Posey and me.

"You guys remember Daisy, right?"
Twee asks.

They stare at Twee blankly.

"Well, Daisy's here to help us!" Twee says.

Now the Pretty Pixies glare at me. "WE DON'T NEED ANY HELP!" they all

shout at once. And in a great hum of pixie dust, they fly away—half in one direction and half in the other.

"Hmm . . . that probably could have gone better," I say.

Chapter Five

Pretty Ugly

I plunk down on a log and sigh.

"How can the Pretty Pixies be so mean to one another?" I ask my friends. "It really makes them not so pretty at all!"

Posey sits next to me and agrees. "Being angry actually makes them pretty ugly."

Then Twee flutters over to my

outstretched finger. "Remember, just because we *look* pretty, doesn't mean we don't ever get upset," she answers sadly. "Sometimes Pretty Pixies need help feeling better too!"

I pull Twee in closer. "But what's making them so mad?" I ask.

Twee sits on my finger and tells us about a Pretty Pixie tradition.

"Every year we have the Pretty Pixie Party," she explains. "It's a magical celebration with fireworks,

cotton candy, and roasted corn. We also sing our special pixie Song of the Forest."

Wow, their party sounds fun! "But how could something so magical turn into something so ugly?" I ask.

Twee shrugs and shakes her head sadly. "I'm not sure," she says. "But something's gone very wrong. I went away for a few days, and when I came back, my pixie sisters were arguing. Now they've been arguing for *days*, and no one will stop being angry long enough to explain how it started."

I lower my finger a little because my whole arm is getting tired from being a perch. "Well, this is positively *terrible*!" I say.

And Posey agrees. "How is anyone supposed to fix the problem if the pixies won't even tell you what's the matter?" he asks.

Twee rests her wee chin in one hand. "I don't know," she says sadly. "But we have to find out soon or our Pretty Pixie Party will be completely ruined!"

"Hmm," I murmur.

"Hmm, what?" Posey asks.

"Well, my grandma Upsy always says that listening solves problems better than yelling."

Posey pulls out a megaphone. "And there sure is a lot of yelling around here!" he adds, hollering loudly.

Twee frowns. "I tried to help them, but they wouldn't let me," she says. "Maybe you and Posey could try."

I nod. "Definitely," I say. "First, I think it might help if Posey and I weren't so big and scary looking."

Twee agrees. So I turn to Posey. "Does imaginary friend dust work on Daisy Dreamers, too?"

Posey's eyes light up. "It does in the WOM!" he says. "Why?"

I hop up from the log. "Because, my friend, you and I need to *get small*!"

Chapter Six

Both Sides of the Story

Posey and I stand side by side.

"Ready?" I say, holding a fistful of imaginary friend dust.

"Ready!" Posey answers.

Then I fling the magical dust in the air, and it drifts down on our heads.

"*Alakazam! Alakazee! Make a pixie out of you and me!*" I shout.

ZIP! ZAP ZOOP! I feel myself shrink

down to pixie size. Posey shrinks too.

"Look at our teeny-tiny hands!" I exclaim. *This is so cool!* "And look, we can even fly like the pixies!" I flutter in a cloud and go *Shoop! Shoop!* this way and that. Posey does the same. This is TMF! Too. Much. Fun. But,

more important, now we are not so
big and scary.

Twee claps her hands in delight.

"You're pixie perfect!" she exclaims.

Then I grab hold of her hand.
"Come on! Let's go talk to those Not-
So-Pretty Pixies!"

Twee flies us to the first Pretty Pixie group. This collection of pixies seems to be the elders. They have white hair and wise eyes. Their leader is named La-di-la, and she agrees to talk to us.

"The Pretty Pixie Party is a time-honored tradition," La-di-la says. "We

have fireworks, cotton candy, and roasted corn, and then we sing our special Song of the Forest. That's the way it's always been, and that's the way it will stay. End of conversation!"

Before I can respond, La-di-la flies away.

"Thanks for telling us how you feel!" I say to her back.

Posey scowls. "More like *yelling* us how you feel," he whispers.

Twee whistles for us to follow. We fly to the other group. These pixies seem younger. They have wild hair and hopeful eyes. Their leader is named Bella. She is shaking her head before I even say one word.

"Why should we talk to you?" she says. "You already talked to La-di-la, which means you're on *her* side!"

I hold my hands out in peace. "No, no, no!" I plead. "We promise to listen to *both* sides!"

Bella looks to her group and then back to us.

"But we're the youngest pixies!" she says. "Nobody listens to the youngest. They all think we have crazy ideas."

I cross my heart. "Age makes no difference," I say. "We want everyone to be happy."

Bella's shoulders relax a little. She agrees to tell her group's side of the story. "The Pretty Pixie Party is very important to us, too, but we'd like to start a *new* tradition with sparkleworks, candy apples, roasted carrots, and the Song of the Forest," she says. "It's time for a change, and we're not going to back down!"

I thank Bella for being

so honest. "Your idea does not sound crazy to me," I say.

Then Posey, Twee, and I have a huddle.

"Well, we've heard both sides of the story," Twee says. "Now what?"

I tap the side of my cheek with one finger to help me think.

"I know that face!" Posey says. "That's Daisy's planning face!"

And, of course, he's right. And an idea has already hatched right in my head.

"I've GOT IT!" I shout. "We need invitations!"

Posey and Twee look at each other and shrug.

"Invitations?" Posey asks with a huff. "Invitations to *what*?"

I sigh dramatically. "Invitations to the *best Pretty Pixie Party ever!*" I say. *Obviously.*

☆ Chapter Seven ☆

Surprise Party!

Twee finds party invitations made from tiny forest flowers, and when you open the flower—*poof!* A burst of glitter pops out. Wow! These are the cutest invitations ever!

"I can't wait to pass them out!" I say.

But first we have to fill in the time and place. Then—*zoomy zoom*

zoom!—we race to each group and hand them out. We spy on the pixies as they open the invitations. It snows glitter *everywhere!*

The leaders from both groups come to visit us. "What are these invitations for?" La-di-la and Bella ask.

"It's a surprise!" I say. "But everyone's going to love it, I promise! Just show up at the Pretty Pixie Meadow at the time on the invitation."

Then we prepare a spectacular party! We set up two long tables with white linen tablecloths. Twee arranges flower centerpieces, and Posey sets up the chairs. Then we fill treat bags with bouncy balls, bead necklaces, party poppers, and rainbow confetti. Last of all, we hang lanterns and twinkle lights in the trees all around.

Then our Pretty Pixie guests begin to arrive and take their seats.

"Welcome, everyone!" I begin. "Welcome to the *best Pretty Pixie Party ever!*" Then I turn to Posey. He nods and flings a handful of imaginary friend dust in the air.

"Yummy-tummies!" Posey shouts. Instantly loads of mouth-watering food float out of the forest and onto the tables.

La-di-la's table gets cotton candy and roasted corn, just like they'd

wanted. Bella's table gets candy apples and roasted carrots, just like they'd wanted. Both tables clap joyfully.

"Hooray for our friend Daisy!" Twee sings. "She found a solution for everyone!"

I take a tiny bow because I feel like a pixie genius.

Then Twee happily flits between tables and puts a little bit of each food on her plate.

"Hey!" shouts La-di-la. "You can't take food from *both* tables!"

Twee looks at her plate.

"And why would you want *their* food," Bella says, "when ours is so much better?"

Some Pretty Pixies at La-di-la's table stand up. "Is not!" they shout.

"Is TOO!" the Bella side shoots back.

Then everyone stands up and begins to shout and point fingers.

"Oh no!" Posey cries. "They are spiraling out of control!"

"And it's all my fault!" Twee wails.

Just like that, our party has gone all Humpty Dumpty. It is totally falling apart.

☆ CHAPTER EIGHT ☆

Listen Up!

But I, Daisy Dreamer, am not going to stand here and let this party be ruined. So I do what everyone else is doing. I yell.

"LISTEN UP! LISTEN UP! HEY! HELLO, YOO-HOO, OUT THERE!" But it's hopeless. Not one pixie listens to me. So I grab hold of Posey.

"Can your imaginary friend dust fix this?" I shout.

Posey shakes his head firmly. "Nope, nope, nope!" he cries. "You can't sprinkle magic on *this*. This is a problem of the mind and the heart, and it can only be solved by listening to one another."

I let go of Posey. *Then how can I get these Pixies' attention? I wonder.* I have to cover my ears to hear myself think. Wait, covering my ears gives me an idea!

"Posey, may I borrow some of your magical dust?"

Posey digs in his fur and hands me a fistful of dust. Then I race over to the tables and grab one firework and one sparklework. I sprinkle the imaginary friend dust on both skyrockets and shout, "Dazzle, snazzle, sparkle, shine!"

The skyrockets launch into the air and explode at the very same time. Fountains of glittery light bloom in the sky. Everyone stops arguing to watch the colorful lights.

"*Ooooooooh!*" all the Pretty Pixies exclaim. "*Aaaaaaaah!*"

"It is magnificent!" La-di-la says, clapping.

"That is the most beautiful display I've ever seen!" Bella adds. "How did you do it?"

I pick up another sparklework and another firework and crisscross them. "I blended both of your fireworks!" I say. "And together, they made something *spectacular!*"

A murmur of wonder comes from both tables.

"The same thing can work for this party if you'll let it," I explain. "It doesn't have to be one way or the other. You can share your ideas and have a Pixie Party more beautiful than ever! Starting right now."

The Pretty Pixies look around the tables at one another and begin to smile, and some nod their heads.

"Well, those candy apples do look delicious," La-di-la says, and takes one from the candy apple platter.

Bella helps herself to cotton candy. "I have room in my heart for cotton candy *and* candy apples!" she says.

Then everyone helps themselves to food from both sides of the celebration.

"I'd like to propose a toast!" I say. We all raise our treats. "To a mix of old and new traditions!"

"Hear! Hear!" the pixies chant.

"And to listening to one another's ideas!" I add.

Then we tap treats, and everyone begins to eat—except Posey. He sets off more fireworks and sparkleworks. And we watch the sparkly blossoms bloom over the WOM.

Then the Pretty Pixies sing the Song
of the Forest:

"We come to sing together,
underneath the Pixie trees
With thanks for all our blessings
and friends and family. . . ."

I try to sing along, but the world begins to spin. Faster and faster it goes, until I swirl right out of the WOM. . . .

A Terrible Mistake

THUNK! I land on my classroom floor—smack on my bottom! *Oof!* I'm back to my normal size again.

Well, at least I landed right side up! I think as I climb into my chair.

The classroom is still empty, and I wonder how long I have been gone. Then I notice that Gabby left her bright pink pencil bag across the table. It has

her name on it in big sky-blue letters. I've never liked it before because it was hers, but now I think it's kind of pretty.

Gabby's bag reminds me of what happened earlier in the day. I remember how nice Gabby was when she helped me this morning.

And then—*gulp*. I think of how *mean* I was when I shouted at her after Carol blinded me with light from her watch. Wow. I blamed Gabby without even listening to her side of the story! Maybe she wasn't helping Carol. And what if maybe she wasn't even making fun of me.

And who knows? Maybe she even saw *Twee*! Wait a sec. *That* must be who she saw on my head this morning! Oh no!

I have made a terrible mistake.

Am I just like the Not-So-Pretty Pixies?

I should have given Gabby a chance to explain what happened before I yelled at her. Maybe I didn't need to be angry at all!

I klunk my head back on my desk and moan.

And then I hear the classroom door creak open.

"Daisy?" I hear someone say.

CHAPTER TEN

Thumbs-Up

I lift my head from the table and see Gabby Gaburp standing in the door-way. She looks a little unsure about talking to me. I guess I can't blame her!

Gabby slowly walks into the room and points to our table. "Um, I left my pencil bag, and I just came to get it. That's all," she says.

I pick it up and hand it to her.

"Are you in trouble, Daisy?" Gabby asks.

"Probably a little trouble," I tell her as she clutches her bag. "But I kinda deserve it."

Our eyes lock.

"I'm really sorry for yelling at you earlier," I say. "I didn't listen to your side of the story, and that wasn't fair."

Gabby studies my face to see if I'm faking. "Umm . . . that's okay."

I smile a little. "It's like sparkleworks and fireworks," I say. "When you mix them together, you get something really beautiful."

I can tell Gabby has no idea what I'm talking about, but she nods slowly, like she's trying to understand. And for a moment I think maybe I am a firework and Gabby is a sparklework, and then we don't seem so different after all.

"You are a little crazy, Daisy Dreamer," she says. But the way she says it isn't mean, and she even smiles a teeny-tiny bit.

And even though Gabby doesn't know anything about the WOM, I think she might sort of understand.

"I'll see you tomorrow," she says as she turns to leave.

"See ya tomorrow," I say.

As Gabby walks toward the door I see my mom and Mr. Roberts. They've been watching us. Mom smiles and gives me a big thumbs-up—she heard my apology, and I know I did the right thing.

Then I sling my backpack over my shoulders, and before I leave the classroom, I look back. The afternoon sun is streaming through the window. And there, in the sunbeam, I can see Twee, Bella, and La-di-la holding hands and waving. The Pretty Pixies are all pretty again.

And I feel kind of pretty inside too.

Check out Daisy Dreamer's next adventure!

#5

Daisy Dreamer

THE Ice Castle

By Holly Anna   Illustrated by Genevieve Santos

WHOOSH!

A gust of wind whips the covers off my warm, snuggly bed. Does the wind want to play hide-and-seek? I feel around for sheets and blankets. I am like a grumpy caterpillar that wants to stay inside her cocoon. I tug the covers over my head.

SWOOSH!

The wind steals them again!

"BAAAAH!" I cry as I jerk the covers back over me. Sir Pounce attacks the ripples in my blanket. *"STOP!"* Then I scrunch up in a ball to keep warm. It's freezing in here. And, wait, *why* is there *wind* in my *bedroom*?

I peek out from under my covers and do a double blink. *Am I dreaming?* I wonder. Or maybe my eyeballs are playing tricks on me! Because . . .

It's *snowing!*

In. My. Room.

And there is an *igloo*!

On. My. Floor.

And someone is crawling out of the igloo's tunnel right now, and I know just who it is! Posey! My imaginary friend!

"HAPPY SNOW DAY!" he shouts, a proud smile on his face. I rub my eyes and smile back at him. Only Posey could make it snow in my room. Then my imaginary friend hops to the window.

"It's snowing outside, too!" he exclaims.

Excerpt from *The Ice Castle*